Sweet Coco
Dessert with Dad

By Jake Pérez
Illustrated By Sarah Watson

Para
Mami y Papi
I love you

While Coco's mom goes to work at her magical chocolate shop
Coco spends time with her dad -
She lovingly calls him Pop

write

Pop does the same things every day:

read

bake

and play

3

He writes articles and books
About traveling to fantastical places,
Sharing recipes from his favorite cooks.

Don't Settle... Be Chewy!
Getting Your Just Desserts

here, there, & ·ever·ywhe.

COME ON, GET MAPPY AN ATLAS

Lately, he's been writing about when he was little.
In some of his old pictures, he seems so tiny and brittle.

"I love this one," he told Coco.
"I remember having so much fun.
I'm baking with my dear abuelita-
A dessert called flan."

"Yummy! Is flan hard to make?"
"Not really," he told her, "just mix and bake."

"Your grandmother - your abuelita - brought the recipe
with her from Cuba, her homeland."
"Cuba?" Coco asked. "Is that far?"
"Sort of," Pop replied.
"You can't get there by car."

"She traveled here long before you came to be,
   From that island paradise
Full of people shaking their hips to an infectious beat -
   Dancing salsa, mambo and the cha cha cha
   Forgetting about the tropical heat.

8

Every Sunday my abuelita's family would gather for a feast
Featuring typical dishes like arroz con pollo - chicken with yellow rice
It gets its golden color from saffron, a reddish-colored spice.

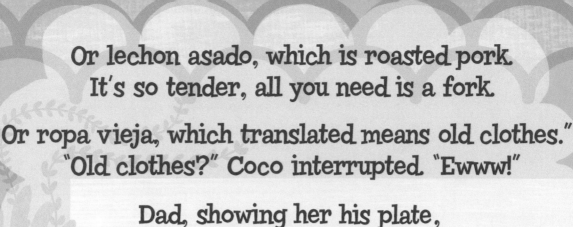

Or lechon asado, which is roasted pork.
It's so tender, all you need is a fork.

Or ropa vieja, which translated means old clothes."
"Old clothes?" Coco interrupted. "Ewww!"

Dad, showing her his plate,
said, "It only looks like old clothes, my love.
It's ripped-up beef in a delicious tomato stew.

Then, the grand finale-
Wrapping up the meal to perfection-
An almost endless dessert selection!

Abuelita and her 3 sisters each had their sweet specialty
One sister would make pasteles de guayaba,
Flaky pastries filled with a fruit called guava

Another sister would make a creamy pudding
as light as air called natilla
Made with vanilla or, in Spanish, vainilla

Another sister would make arroz con leche
A gloopy, dreamy rice pudding
She'd patiently stir and stir over a stove,
then chill it Saturday night
So that by Sunday, it'd be just right

arroz
con leche

natilla

pasteles de guayaba

But my favorite was - and still is - abuelita's homemade flan!
Everyone who tasted it fell in love
with her special, creamy custard, especially me...
So she shared her secret recipe."

"Can you teach me how to make it, Pop?" Coco asked.
"Pretty please?"
"Nothing would make me happier, little one...
Sharing my abuelita's secret with you sounds like fun."

Recipe

Flan de Leche
❁
Milk Flan

To make the caramel:
  2 tablespoons water
  6 tablespoons sugar

Stir the water and sugar together in a 3" deep flan pan. Heat on stovetop on medium heat for about 10 minutes, or until golden brown. Coat the bottom and sides of the pan with the caramel while it's still warm. Allow it to set.

To make the flan

1- 14 ounce can sweetened condensed milk
1- 12 ounce can evaporated milk
1 cup half and half
5 eggs
1 teaspoon vanilla
a pinch of salt

Preheat the oven to 350°.
Combine flan ingredients in a blender. Pour the mixture into the caramel-coated flan pan. Rest the flan pan in a water bath (a larger pan filled with about an inch and a half of water).
Bake for 1 hour.
Allow the pan to cool, then place in the refrigerator from 4 hours to overnight.
Edge the pan with a butterknife and flip it onto a serving dish.
Keep the pan upside down for a few minutes to allow the caramel to pool onto the flan and the serving dish.
Slice and serve!

"Do we have everything we need, Coco?"
"Yes, Pop," she responded. "We're all set."
"Great! The first step involves making the caramel sauce.

But it's best that I handle this part."
"Why?" asked Coco.
"It's tricky, sticky, and piping hot.
It involves a lot of care and some practice.
Trust me, you'll have plenty of time to try
when you're older, Little Miss.

Here's how you do it:
First, mix the sugar and water
in the flan pan.
Carefully place it on the oven burner.
Turn the oven on to medium heat.
Then, watch the magic unfold
Right there in the flan mold...

The liquid will slowly
change color
to a clear, golden goo."
"Whoa," Coco said
in a state of wonder.
"It's true!"

"Once it's ready," Pop continued, "turn off the burner.
With mitts on, carefully tilt the pan
Around and around
To coat the bottom and sides of the mold.
The caramel will harden
when it's removed from the heat and allowed to get cold.

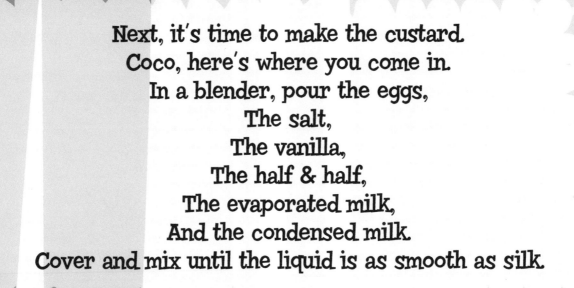

Next, it's time to make the custard.
Coco, here's where you come in.
In a blender, pour the eggs,
The salt,
The vanilla,
The half & half,
The evaporated milk,
And the condensed milk.
Cover and mix until the liquid is as smooth as silk.

Pour the mix into
the caramel-covered pan.

Then, carefully place the pan
in the shallow water bath.

Now for a little bit of math...
Make sure the oven is set
to 350 degrees.

Place the water bath-pan comb
in the oven for 60 minutes."

"That's an HOUR!"

Coco sighed.

"Waiting is definitely the toughest part."
"I agree," Pop replied. "Patience, sweetheart.

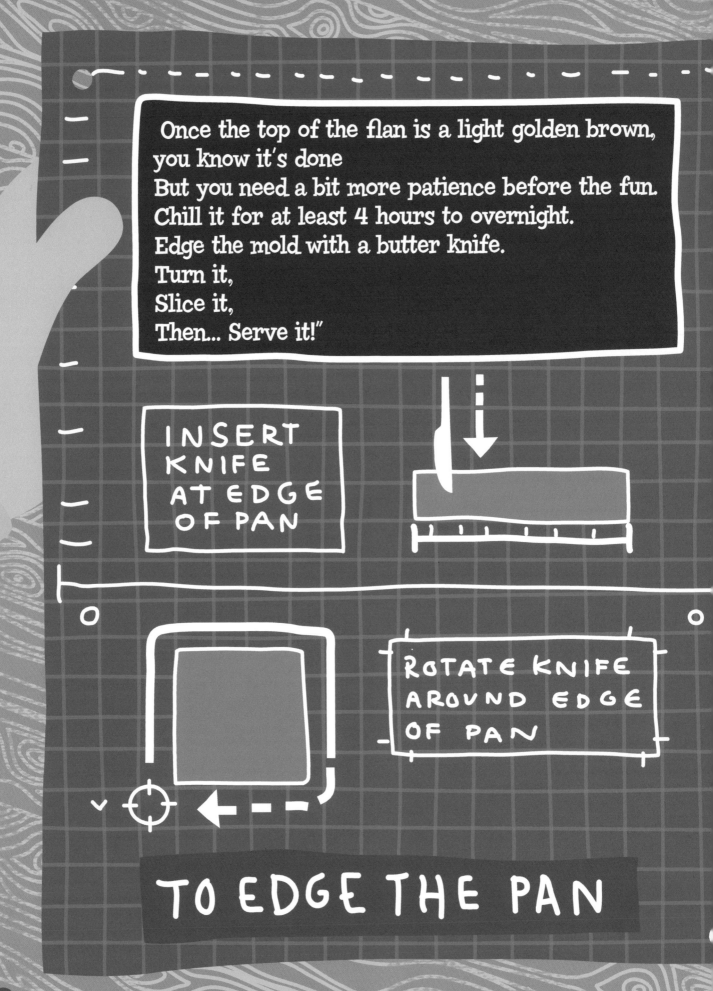

Once the top of the flan is a light golden brown, you know it's done
But you need a bit more patience before the fun.
Chill it for at least 4 hours to overnight.
Edge the mold with a butter knife.
Turn it,
Slice it,
Then... Serve it!"

INSERT KNIFE AT EDGE OF PAN

ROTATE KNIFE AROUND EDGE OF PAN

TO EDGE THE PAN

TO FLIP THE FLAN

PLACE PLATE ON TOP OF FLAN PAN

FLIP!

LET SAUCE POOL ON PLATE, THEN GENTLY LIFT PAN

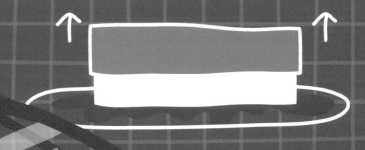

"Oh, no!
That means I'll have to wait even longer,
because it needs to cool...
And I'm already starting to drool!"
"Not this time," Pop replied,
"While you were sleeping, I made...

measure

heat
&
coat sides

mix & pour

SUGAR

ONLY the wheat vanilla

Condensed MILK

sweet dairy
YUM EVAPORATED MILK
FARMS

bake

wait

A miniature one
Just for you!
I treasured my time with my abuelita...
She shared her time, her love, and her special recipe with me...
Now, I share them with you!"

"Thank you, Pop," Coco replied gratefully,
"But I have a surprise to share, too."
Handing him a spoon, she said, "This isn't a flan for one.
It's a flan for two: Me and You!"

the
end

CPSIA information can be obtained at www.ICGtesting.com
Printed in the USA
BVIW12n2012301016
466235BV00001B/1